The Best
Snowman

12

U16

First published in 2000
This edition published in 2001 by
Franklin Watts
96 Leonard Street
London
EC2A 4XD

Franklin Watts Australia
45–51 Huntley Street
Alexandria
NSW 2015

Text © Margaret Nash 2000
Illustration © Jörg Saupe 2000

The rights of Margaret Nash to be identified as the author
and Jörg Saupe as the illustrator of this Work have been
asserted in accordance with the Copyright, Designs and
Patents Act, 1988.

A CIP catalogue record for this book is available
from the British Library.

ISBN 0 7496 3728 5 (hbk)
ISBN 0 7496 4390 0 (pbk)

Series Editor: Louise John
Series Advisor: Dr Barrie Wade
Series Designer: Jason Anscomb

Printed in Hong Kong

The Best Snowman

by Margaret Nash

Illustrated by Jörg Saupe

W
FRANKLIN WATTS
LONDON•SYDNEY

Ravi had never seen snow.
Then, one cold day, it came.

Ravi made a snowman as fat as a barrel.

Then he stuck a saucepan
on its head.

"He's funny," said Mr Jones,
who lived next door.

"Can you make one for me, too?"

"And me," said Mrs Cook.

10

"And us," said Miss Ling and Mr Parry.

"I'll make snowmen for all of you."

13

"One like yours, please,"
said Mr Jones.

"As fat as a barrel!"

The snowman was a very funny shape.

But Mr Jones was pleased.

"A tall, thin one, please,"
said Miss Ling.

The snowman was so tall
and thin, it couldn't stand up.
But Miss Ling was pleased.

"I'd like a snow-woman, please," said Mrs Cook.

The hat was much too big
for the snow-woman.
But Mrs Cook was pleased.

Ravi came to the last house.

"Oh, dear!" he said.

"A teeny-weeny snowman, please," said Mr Parry.

"They're the best."

So, Ravi made a snowman the size of a snowball.

"Why is he the best?" asked Ravi.

Mr Parry took the teeny-weeny snowman ...

and put him in the freezer
with the frozen peas.

"He's the best snowman because he won't melt," said Mr Parry.

And he didn't!

Leapfrog has been specially designed to fit the requirements of the National Literacy Strategy. It offers real books for beginning readers by top authors and illustrators.

There are 25 Leapfrog stories to choose from: